The LoveBugs Welcome Party

Written by Joanne Grady

Illustrated by Adam Turner

Dedication

To my favorite little LoveBugs, Ashlynne, Bailee, Simon J. and big brother, Josh. Also to Ann V. Zeidman and Sandy Daulton Zeidman, who, with effortless joy and compassion for others, are proof that grown up LoveBugs exist, too.

Acknowledgements

Heartfelt thanks to my children, who giggled and embraced the games of silly sentences and stories we created when they were young. To Carol Hirsh Blechman who inspires others with her love for reading children's stories. And lastly, gratitude for my Editor, Naomi C. Rose and my Illustrator, Adam Turner; your brilliant talent and expertise truly make the LoveBugs come alive.

~~~~~~~~~~~~~~~~~~

ISBN: 978-0-9990075-1-8

Library of Congress Control Number: 2017942133

Book design by Naomi C. Rose, www.ncrdesigns.com

Text set in: Bangla MN

Grady Bunch Books, LLC
www.gradybunchbooks.com

Printed in USA

The sun wakes with a splash of color.

3

Fingers of sunlight stretch and wave hello to the LoveBugs.
They all pop up in happy reply, except for Ashlynne.

She snuggles under her leaf. "Mommy. I'm still sleeping,"
she mumbles. "I don't want the light on."

Swoosh! DaddyBug scoops her up, tickling her with wake-up kisses. "I love you like crazy. I'm happy you're here. I could kiss you all day, sweet baby dear!"

"Daddy, stop." She giggles.

6

"Mommy," calls Ashlynne, "J.J. says a new BabyBug is coming soon. Is it our turn? Can we take it home? Pleeease? I'll share all my toys. I really, really love BabyBugs."

"I know you do," says MommyBug. "But it's still not our turn."

With a huff, Ashlynne pokes at the berries in her bowl.
Grrrroar, says her tummy. She nibbles a berry, daydreaming
about a new BabyBug.

Thump-thump, thump-thump.

Ahhhh. BabyBugs always make her heart go *thump-thump.* "I have an idea!" She flaps her wings, gobbles up the berries, and reaches for her crayons. "I need to go color!"

Ashlynne skips outside to hunt for a leaf to color. Her ears jiggle at a happy sound.

Plop! Plop! Plop! Morning dewdrops tumble down the top of the acorn houses.

Splash! They land in the window planters below where thirsty Bugs slurp up the water.

11

Ashlynne joins her friends, all a-flutter.

"Did you hear? Did you hear?" yells Olivia. "The new baby LoveBug comes *today* and there's a party!" Olivia is always loud because she can't hear very well. Today her loud voice rings with excitement.

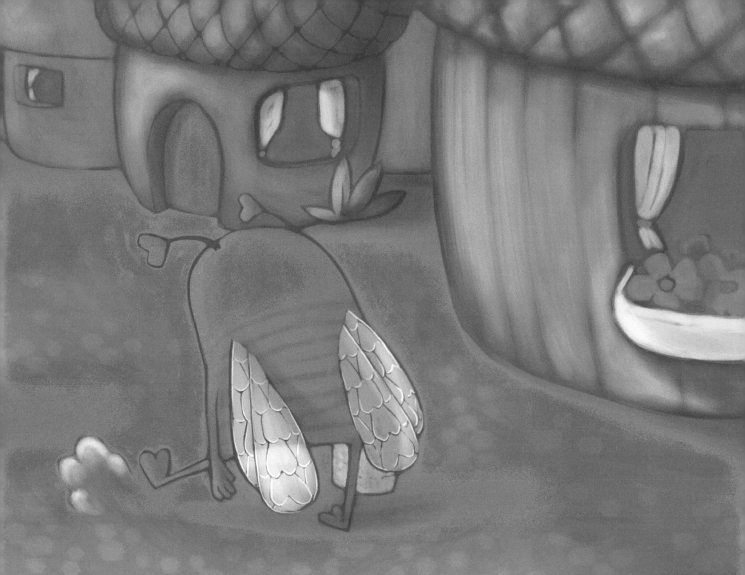

J.J. bounces up and down. "The BabyBug is coming to my house!"

Ashlynne scuffs at the dirt. "No fair," she mutters. "I wished and wished for a new BabyBug."

"I don't know its name yet," says J.J., "and I have to be quiet when he's asleep. And I made a cake with my DaddyBug."

"I hope it's chocolate," says Kyle. "And I hope he likes this baby blanket." *Snip. Snip.* He clips around a very large leaf.

Layla whispers, "We know you want a BabyBug too, Ashlynne. More than anything."

"Yeah," hollers Olivia, "even more than chocolate cake."

"I just love BabyBugs," sighs Ashlynne. *Thump-thump* goes her heart. "Oh! My picture."

She snatches a leaf, digs into her crayons and gets busy.

"Come on, Olivia," nudges Layla, "let's pick flowers."

THUMP

THUMP

THUMP

They finish just in time: *THUMP-THUMP, THUMP-THUMP,*
THUMP-THUMP. A very loud heartbeat makes them all jump.

17

"Hooray!" yells Olivia. "That's Georgia's heartbeat. It's time for the party."

"I better get the cake," cries J.J.

Ashlynne scribbles big letter 'A' on her leaf. "Now the BabyBug will know it's from me."

The young Bugs scurry in a hurry to join all the bustling LoveBugs at the Big Rock.

J.J.and his DaddyBug parade by with the cake. Ashlynne sniffs deeply. *Kaboomp.* She topples over onto another LoveBug. "Yummm! Choooocolaate!" they giggle.

19

She pops up with arms and wings waggling. Their leader, Felipe, climbs the Big Rock. He nods at Georgia. "We're ready."

THUMP-THUMP, THUMP-THUMP. Georgia's loud heartbeat quiets the chatter. All the bug eyes stare at the Big Rock.

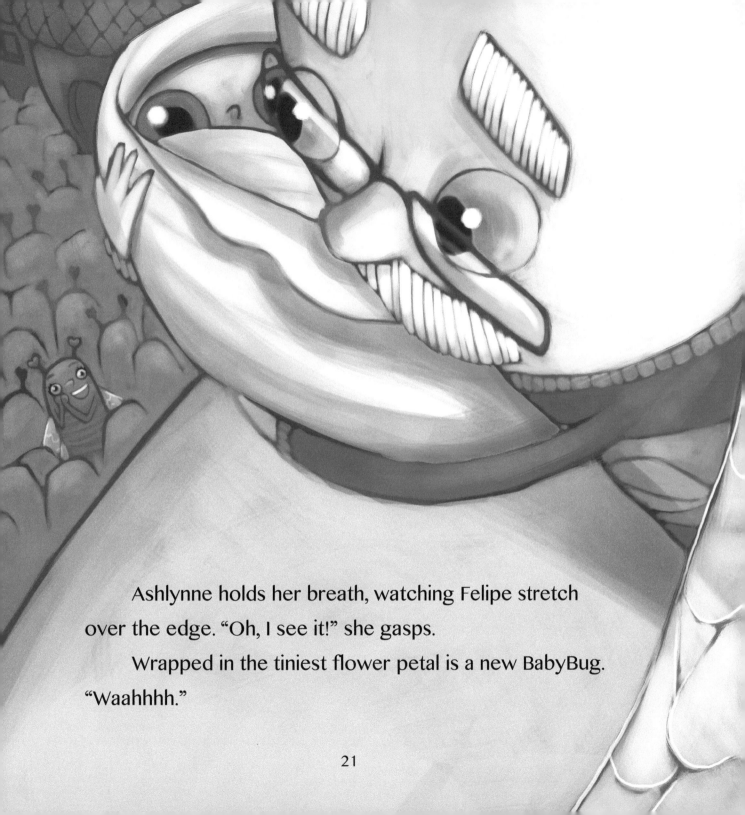

Ashlynne holds her breath, watching Felipe stretch over the edge. "Oh, I see it!" she gasps.

Wrapped in the tiniest flower petal is a new BabyBug. "Waahhhh."

Felipe spots the name tag. "Here is what we waited for today. Everybody, welcome Simon J."

"Welcome, Simon J!" The LoveBugs sing and dance.

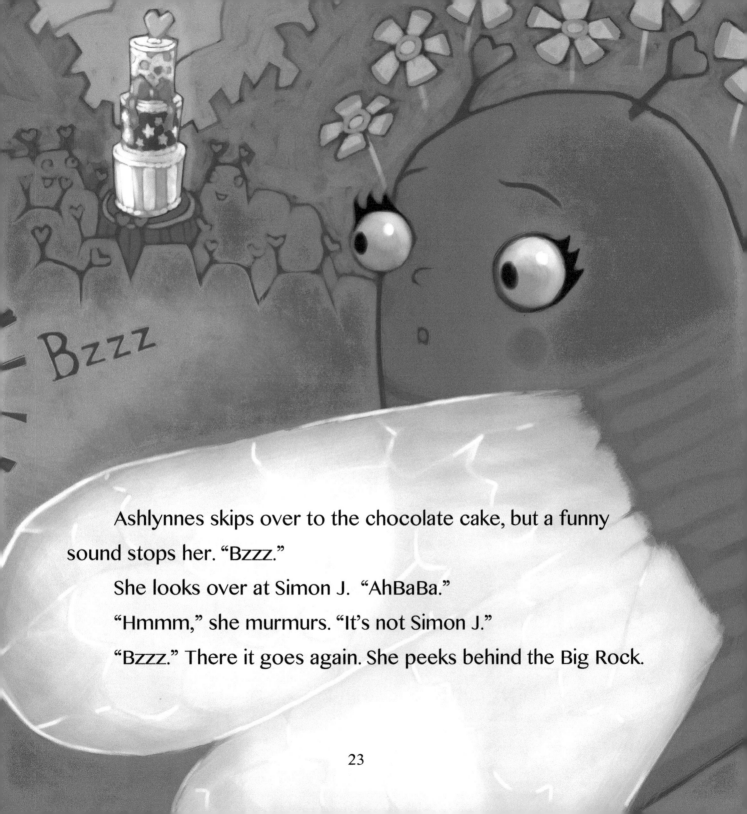

Bzzz

Ashlynnes skips over to the chocolate cake, but a funny sound stops her. "Bzzz."

She looks over at Simon J. "AhBaBa."

"Hmmm," she murmurs. "It's not Simon J."

"Bzzz." There it goes again. She peeks behind the Big Rock.

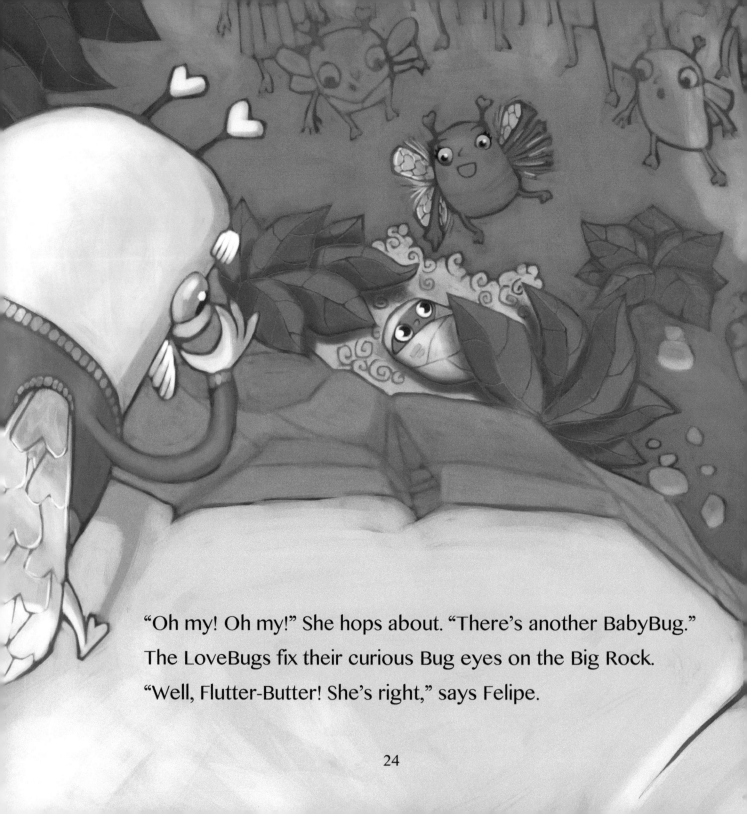

"Oh my! Oh my!" She hops about. "There's another BabyBug."
The LoveBugs fix their curious Bug eyes on the Big Rock.
"Well, Flutter-Butter! She's right," says Felipe.

24

"Bzzz," replies a small voice.

Ashlynne slowly lifts the BabyBug up to Felipe. He wipes his glasses to read the name tag.

25

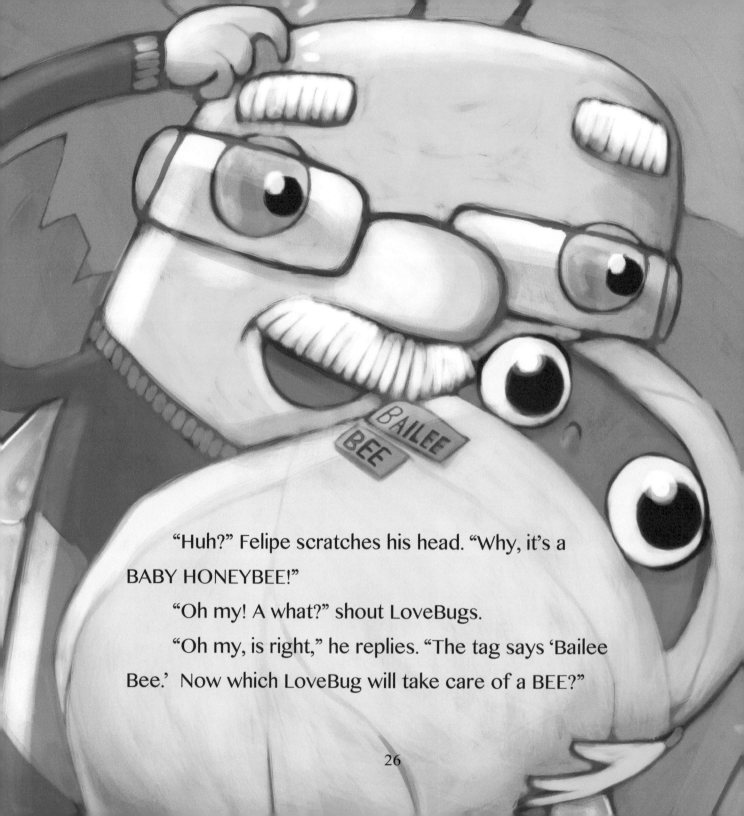

"Huh?" Felipe scratches his head. "Why, it's a BABY HONEYBEE!"

"Oh my! A what?" shout LoveBugs.

"Oh my, is right," he replies. "The tag says 'Bailee Bee.' Now which LoveBug will take care of a BEE?"

Ashlynne flaps and waves. "I'll do it!" I really, really want a sister. Look! I colored a picture. She can have it. I'll share all my toys! *Please?* I'm using Please."

27

Felipe turns to the LoveBugs. "I think Ashlynne will be a terrific sister for Bailee Bee. Do you?"

"Yes, Yes!" they reply.

"Bzzz," says Bailee.

"AhBaBa," says Simon J.

"Yippeee," says Ashlynne, snuggling up to Bailee. "Oh,
I love you like crazy. I'm happy you're here. I could kiss you
all day, little Bailee Bee dear."

Thump-thump, thump-thump goes Ashlynne's heart.

29

The welcome party continues with chatter and chocolate cake until the sun lays down for a rest. Gentle moonlight guides sleepy LoveBugs back home.

30

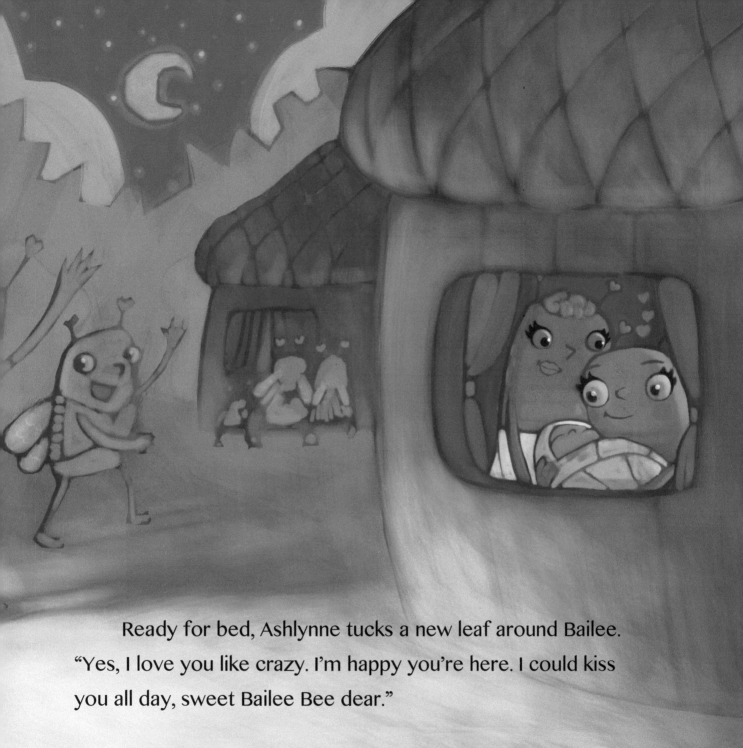

Ready for bed, Ashlynne tucks a new leaf around Bailee.
"Yes, I love you like crazy. I'm happy you're here. I could kiss
you all day, sweet Bailee Bee dear."

And inside every acorn house, LoveBug hearts overflow with love for Simon J. and Bailee Bee. *Thump-thump. Thump-thump. Thump-thump.*

Can you guess whose heart thumps loudest of all?

CPSIA information can be obtained
at www.ICGtesting.com
Printed in the USA
BVHW022350250219
541176BV00001B/5/P